Licensed exclusively to Top That Publishing Ltd
Tide Mill Way, Woodbridge, Suffolk, IP12 1AP, UK
www.topthatpublishing.com
Copyright © 2015 Monika Filipina Trzpil
All rights reserved
0 2 4 6 8 9 7 5 3 1
Printed and bound in China

Written and illustrated by Monika Filipina Trzpil

ISBN 978-1-78445-245-2

A catalogue record for this book is available from the British Library

'To all clumsy bears'

The Bear who loved to Dance

by
Monika Filipina Trzpil

Bear loved to dance.

He practised in his bedroom every day.

Bear wanted to dance with the other animals, but he was very clumsy.

Bear tried ballet.
But all the giraffes just
laughed at him.

Twirl ...

Whirl ...

Bend ...

Thud!

Thud!

Stomp!

'You're not graceful enough for ballet,' they mocked.

So Bear tried breakdance.

Break, break ...

B-b-b-b-break ...

Bear tried tap dance too.

Tap ...

Tap ...

Tap ...

But the rhinos grumbled at Bear. 'You're not quick enough for tap dance!' they scoffed.

Then Bear tried swing …

... but Zebra wasn't happy.

'You're too strong for swing!' she cried.

Bear even tried

synchronized swimming ...

But the tortoises laughed at Bear too.

Poor Bear couldn't seem to do anything right …

Tweet!
Tweet!
Tweet!

Until one day he noticed a poster ...

Bear decided to take part in the competition.

When the day came he was
very nervous.

But Bear ...

was ...

simply ...

a m a z i n g!

The judges loved Bear's dancing.
'**10** out of **10**!' they cheered.

Bear won first place in the competition
   and he was given a shiny gold medal.

Slide!

And all the other animals ...

Wobble!

learnt that dancing on ice ...

Twizzle!

Whoops!

Slip!

... was not easy

at all!